F

T

TAYLOR, ANDREW

THE PRIVATE NOSE

DEMCO

THE
PRIVATE NOSE

"My . . . my curtains weren't closed all the way," cried
Amelia. "Suddenly I could see this white shape."

THE PRIVATE NOSE

by

ANDREW TAYLOR

illustrated by

EMANUEL SCHONGUT

CANDLEWICK PRESS
CAMBRIDGE, MASSACHUSETTS

First U.S. edition 1993
First published in Great Britain in 1989 by
Walker Books Ltd., London.

Library of Congress Cataloging-in-Publication Data:

Taylor, Andrew, 1951- The private nose/Andrew Taylor:
illustrated by Emanuel Schongut.

Summary: Jack Watson and his new neighbor Saturday Holmes
investigate a case of a missing teddy bear and
two other mysteries.
[1. Mystery and detective stories.]
I. Schongut, Emanuel, ill. II. Title.
PZ7.T2117Pr 1993 [Fic]—dc20 92-53016
ISBN 1-56402-135-1

10 9 8 7 6 5 4 3 2 1

Printed in the U.S.A.

Candlewick Press
2067 Massachusetts Avenue
Cambridge, Massachusetts 02140

For Sarah

CONTENTS

*The lion's huge teeth crunched
through the buffalo bones.*

THE CASE
OF THE
MISSING BEAR

The mighty jaws crashed together. The lion's huge teeth crunched through the buffalo bones as if they were crackers. The lion swallowed.

"Jack, dear," said Mrs. Watson. "Don't eat with your mouth open. I don't want to see your cornflakes. Or hear them."

"Has anyone seen Rusty?" Mr. Watson said. He spread some jam on his toast. "That cat treats this house like a hotel."

Jack put down his spoon. "She's asleep in the yard. Can I have some toast now?"

His mother nodded. Jack put two pieces on his plate. His father raised his eyebrows.

"I'm not being greedy," Jack said quickly. "The other piece is for L.T."

This was an old joke. L.T. stood for Little Teddy. When Jack was younger, he used to take L.T. everywhere. According to Jack, L.T. was always hungry.

"Our new neighbors are moving in today," Mrs. Watson said. "Mrs. Patel told me."

"Do they have any children?" Jack asked.

"I think there are two — a girl and a boy. But they may not be the same age as you." She looked across the kitchen table at Mr. Watson. "You'll never guess what their last name is. Holmes!"

Mr. Watson laughed. "So the Holmeses and the Watsons will be living next door to one another!"

"Why's that funny, Dad?"

"There are some famous stories about a Holmes and a Watson." Jack's father looked at his watch. "I'll have to run or I'll be late for work. I'll put the trash can out front."

It was Thursday — the trash collectors always came on Thursday.

After breakfast Jack went upstairs to his bedroom. It was a little room at the front of the house. L.T. was sitting on the windowsill. He was wearing a gray wool hat and a blue sweater.

Jack played with his train, but he kept an eye on the road as well. He wanted to be the first to see the Holmeses.

The house next door had been empty for six weeks. Before that an old couple had lived there. The Holmeses sounded much more interesting.

A red car and a blue-and-orange moving van pulled up outside.

As Jack and L.T. watched, four people got out of the car. The man had pink-and-white skin. The woman had dark brown skin. The boy and the girl had light brown skin. The boy was so old that he was nearly grown-up, and the girl looked a little older than Jack.

Jack enjoyed watching the movers. They carried beds and sofas and armchairs as if they were as light as feathers. He didn't see much of the new neighbors because they were inside the house. After a while the boy rode off on a bicycle with racing handlebars.

The girl came out into the yard for a few minutes. She looked up at the Watsons' house. Jack ducked back and moved L.T. from the windowsill. He didn't want the girl to think he was babyish. After all, he didn't really play with L.T. anymore.

The van drove away long before dinner time. Mrs. Watson said she was going to say hello to the Holmeses and see if they needed anything.

Jack went with her. By mistake, he brought L.T. downstairs as well.

"Are you taking L.T.?" his mother said in surprise.

Jack felt embarrassed. Of course he wasn't. He left L.T. on the front porch, on the shelf where the empty bottles went.

The Holmeses' house was like the Watsons' but the other way around, as if it were in a mirror. Mr. Holmes opened the door. Behind him, Mrs. Holmes was kneeling on the floor with her head in a packing case. She pulled out her head and smiled at them.

Mrs. Watson introduced herself and Jack.

"Holmes and Watson!" Mr. Holmes grinned. "I bet the police will want us to help them!"

Everyone laughed. Jack joined in. He wished someone would explain what was so funny about Holmes and Watson.

The Watsons didn't stay long because Mr. and Mrs. Holmes were very busy unpacking. Mrs. Watson invited the whole family to come for coffee on Saturday morning. Jack felt disappointed because the girl wasn't there.

Jack left L.T. on the front porch, on the
shelf where the empty bottles went.

When they got home, Jack went right to the end of the backyard to play soccer. He kicked the ball very hard against the wall, and it bounced back at him. It was almost as good as having someone to play with.

He kicked the ball twelve times, and twelve times it came bouncing back. But on the thirteenth kick, his foot slipped. The ball shot up in the air and sailed over the wall into the Holmeses' backyard.

Jack knew what to do. He climbed up the apple tree and onto the top of the wall. It was a short drop down to next-door's compost heap; then there was a shorter drop to the ground. No one could see you from the house.

Just as Jack was about to jump, a voice said, "What do you think you're doing?"

It was the girl. She was standing by the toolshed and she wasn't smiling. In her hand was Jack's ball.

15

Jack knew what to do. He climbed up the apple tree and onto the top of the wall.

"Hello," Jack said. "Sorry, I kicked my ball over."

"Catch!" She threw it to him. "What's your name?"

"I'm Jack," Jack said. "What's yours?"

"Saturday Holmes."

"Saturday? But that's what comes before Sunday. It's a *day*."

"It can also be a person's name. *Everyone* knows that."

"Oh," Jack thought for a minute. "Do you want to come and play soccer?"

"No." Saturday sniffed. "I've got something more important to do."

She turned and walked away. Jack climbed down the apple tree.

Oh dear, he thought, I messed that up. She must have thought I was making fun of her name.

He wondered what she had to do that was so

very important.

Playing soccer wasn't as much fun as it had been. Jack kicked the ball into the rhubarb and went back to the house. He wished that Saturday had been nicer. He was getting bored with playing by himself. That was the trouble with school vacations.

Jack decided to take L.T. upstairs. He walked around to the front yard. The trash can had been emptied, and its lid was lying on the path.

But the bear wasn't on the shelf on the porch.

Jack ran into the house, down the hall, and into the kitchen.

"Mom," he said. "Did you take L.T. upstairs?"

His mother was sitting at the table, paying some bills. "Isn't he on the porch?" she said.

"No. I've looked there."

"Well, he can't have gone far. Maybe he fell off the shelf. Maybe you took him into the yard when we got back from next door. Maybe you — "

"But I *didn't!*" Jack said.

Jack looked on the porch. He looked in the yard. He even looked in the house. But there was no sign of L.T.

He went back to the front yard. He couldn't help worrying about L.T., though of course he was much too old for toys like that. He took out a tissue from the pocket of his overalls.

"What's up?" someone said behind him.

Jack looked around, hiding the tissue behind his back.

Saturday was leaning on the wooden fence between the front yards of their houses. The fence was much lower than the brick wall in the back.

"I've lost . . . something," Jack said. "It doesn't matter."

Saturday looked hard at him. "You sound like

Saturday was leaning on the wooden fence
between the front yards of their houses.

it matters. What is it?"

"It's L.T.," Jack said before he could stop himself. He was so miserable that he forgot that Saturday might think him babyish. "He's my bear."

"Maybe I can help," Saturday said. "I'm good at solving mysteries. I've got the Holmes Nose."

Jack stared at Saturday's face. Her nose looked very ordinary to him. It was straight and big.

"How can your nose help?" he asked.

"Because it's the Holmes Nose, of course." Saturday climbed over the fence and stood besides him. "Haven't you heard of Sherlock Holmes?"

Jack said that he thought he might have, but he wasn't sure.

"He was the greatest detective who ever lived," Saturday said proudly. "He was the brother of my grandfather's grandfather. I'm a detective too. I decided to start today. That's why I didn't want to play soccer."

"Oh." Jack felt a little better.

"Now," Saturday said briskly, "you'd better take me to the scene of the crime."

"To the what?" Jack said.

"Where the bearnapping took place." Saturday tapped her nose. "L.T. must have been stolen. I can smell it. I need to look for clues."

Jack showed her the porch. Saturday got down on her knees and examined every inch of the floor.

"Look what I've found!" she said. "It was between the doormat and the wall. Does it belong to the missing bear?"

She held up L.T.'s gray wool hat.

"Yes, it does!" Jack shouted. "That proves he's been stolen!"

"Shh!" Saturday said. "I can't hear myself think."

She looked very closely at both sides of the hat.

"Aha!" she said. "Look at this, Jack. It's an important clue."

A red hair glowed against the gray of the hat.

"What does it mean?" Jack said excitedly.

Saturday looked down her nose at him. "It means that whoever took L.T. almost certainly had red hair. Who do you know with red hair?"

Jack thought hard. "Miss Lines," he said. "She's my teacher at school. And there's Justin Badweather. He's in the grade above me. He's horrible. But he's away at his uncle's. And then there's the policeman who lives down the road — he's got a red moustache."

Saturday said, "I can't see why a policeman or a teacher would want to steal L.T. It's a pity that Justin isn't here. He sounds like a good suspect." She looked down the path toward the gate and rubbed her nose. "But luckily I've got another idea."

"Tell me," Jack demanded.

Saturday shook her head. "Not yet. Not until we know more. We need a witness. Do any of the neighbors look out of the window a lot?"

"Mrs. Grump does," Jack said. "She's the lady who lives across the street, next door to the Patels. She's always sewing in her front room. Look, she's there now."

They stared at the house opposite. It was freshly painted and had a very neat yard. To the right of the door was a big bow window. Mrs. Grump was sitting there with a sewing machine on the table beside her.

"Come on," said Saturday. "We'll go and question her."

"But . . . she might be busy," Jack said.

Mrs. Grump didn't like children because

they dropped candy wrappers over the fence into her yard. Sometimes she chased them with her broom.

"Are you scared?" Saturday asked. "You have to be brave to be a detective."

"No . . . " Jack didn't want to admit that he was scared. He thought of something interesting about Mrs. Grump. "She's cruel. Once I saw her throw a stone at Rusty."

"She threw a stone at Rusty?" Saturday said. "Who's that?"

"Not *who* — *what*," Jack said. He saw a chance to get back at her. Rusty's the name of our cat. *Everyone* knows that."

"If you ask me," Saturday said, "it's a silly name for a cat." Saturday started walking down the path. "Come on," she said over her shoulder to Jack. "You're not a scaredy-cat, are you?"

Jack caught up to her on the sidewalk. They

crossed the street together and opened Mrs. Grump's front gate. It was made of iron and painted shiny black. Mrs. Grump's concrete path was so clean it almost sparkled. Even her trash can looked as if it had a bath every night.

"She's watching us," Jack whispered.

"I know," Saturday said loudly. "*I'm* not afraid."

She marched up the path and pushed the doorbell. It chimed a little tune. She waited for a minute and pushed the bell again.

Suddenly the door opened.

"That's enough of your nonsense!" screeched Mrs. Grump. She was a big fat woman in a black dress. "You'll wear out my chimes if you ring them more than once. Well! Come on! What is it?"

"I'm Saturday Holmes," Saturday said. "We just moved in."

"Saturday?" Mrs. Grump grunted. "Call that a name?"

"She's watching us," Jack whispered.
"I know," Saturday said loudly. "I'm not afraid."

"Someone stole Jack's bear this morning," Saturday said. "You know, a teddy bear. He left it on the porch when he came to our house. Did you see anyone going up their front path?"

"No. No one at all," Mrs. Grump snapped. She began to close the door.

Saturday put her foot in front of the door. "You're wrong. At least one person must have gone up there."

"Take your foot away! And don't be smart." Mrs. Grump swelled like a large black balloon.

"I'm not being smart," Saturday said calmly. "When we got here this morning, all the trash cans were full. But when Jack asked me to look at the scene of the . . . at the porch, I mean, their trash can was empty. I bet yours is too. So the trash collectors must have been here."

Jack bit his lip. He had suddenly remembered the trash collectors' truck — a panda and a rabbit dangled from a wire across the radiator.

Perhaps the trash collectors thought L.T. was part of the Watsons' trash. L.T. might now be hanging there as well.

"Pah!" Mrs. Grump said. "Of course the trash collectors came. They always do on Thursday. I wasn't counting people like trash collectors and mailmen."

"What color hair did they have?" Saturday asked.

"What color hair . . . ?" Mrs. Grump swelled a little more. "Pah! I couldn't believe my eyes. The young one had his hair dyed green and blue! The other two have gray hair. At least they're normal."

"Thank you, Mrs. Grump," Saturday said. "Good-bye."

She and Jack walked quickly down the path.

"And don't forget to close the gate after you," Mrs. Grump called after them. "Carefully — or else you'll chip the paint. Pah! Kids! I ask you!"

"Phew!" Jack said when they were back in the Watsons' yard. "I'm glad that's over."

"All in a day's work for a detective," Saturday said.

She put her hands in the pockets of her jeans and went to look at L.T.'s hat. They had left it on the shelf on the porch. Jack followed her.

"Trouble is," she said, "we haven't solved the mystery. All we've done is prove that *no one* could have stolen L.T. The trash collectors had the wrong color hair. The only other people who've been near the porch are you, me, and your mom. Unless your mom's got red hair — "

"No, I don't!"

Mrs. Watson had come around the side of the house, walking silently on the grass. Her hair was dark and short.

"You must be Saturday," she said with a smile. "Jack, haven't you found L.T. yet?"

Jack shook his head. He was beginning to

think that L.T. was lost forever.

"We'll take a look for him after lunch." His mother ruffled Jack's hair. "Cheer up. We'll find him. It seems to be the sort of day for disappearances. I haven't seen Rusty since before breakfast."

"Rusty," Saturday said dreamily. "*Rusty!* Why didn't I think of that before?"

"Are you feeling all right?" Mrs. Watson asked.

"Rusty! What color is your cat?"

"Well, she's a mixture," Mrs. Watson said. "She's kind of orangey — "

"Red!" Jack shouted.

Saturday picked up the gray hat with the red hair. She looked at Jack. "Where does Rusty go when she wants to be alone? Anywhere in particular?"

Jack cleared his throat. This was awkward. Rusty had a special place, but it was a secret.

31

She wasn't supposed to go upstairs.

"Actually," he said, "Rusty sometimes hides under my bed. When no one's looking."

Sometimes Rusty slept on top of the bed. There was no need to mention that.

"Come on," said Saturday. "Where's your room?"

They ran upstairs and looked under the bed. Rusty was lying there, washing L.T. with her tongue. Jack wriggled under the bed and rescued him from between Rusty's paws.

"Is he all right?" Saturday said.

Jack nodded. "Just a little wet."

That afternoon, Saturday and Jack sat side by side on the wall by the apple tree. L.T. was drying out between them.

Jack's mother had explained that Rusty thought L.T. was her kitten, and so she was washing him. Mrs. Watson had given Rusty an old furry mouse that made a much better kitten than L.T. had.

"You were very clever," Jack said.

Saturday modestly said nothing, but he could see that she agreed.

"Was it the Nose that did it?" Jack asked.

"It helped," Saturday said. "By the way, I didn't know your last name was Watson. Not until my parents said it."

"So what?" Jack said.

"Well — Sherlock Holmes had a Watson. He helped with the easy parts. You can help me, if you want."

"With the detecting? Yes, *please*." Jack nearly fell off the wall in his excitement.

Saturday kicked her heels against the bricks. "Most detectives who aren't on the police force call themselves private eyes." She paused and looked at Jack. "But I will call myself the Private Nose."

Behind the small carriage was a small person who was wearing a pink dress and had very long pigtails.

THE CASE
OF THE
LITTLEJOHNS' GHOST

Jack Watson was lying on the grass reading a comic book.

He was in the Holmeses' garden. Saturday Holmes, the great detective, was looking at a woodlouse through her brother's magnifying glass.

Something was squeaking in the distance. Saturday and Jack looked up. The noise grew louder. A small carriage appeared by the front gate. Behind the small carriage was a small person who was wearing a pink dress and had very long pigtails. On the ends of the pigtails were pink ribbons tied with big bows.

"Oh no!" Jack thought. "It's boring old Amelia Littlejohn."

"Hello," Saturday said. She got up and opened the gate.

Amelia wheeled in the carriage. Inside the carriage were her two dolls, Amanda and Miranda. Amelia's eyes were red and her lips were trembling.

"Oh, Saturday," she said. "I need a Private Nose!"

Then she started to cry.

Saturday, who called herself the Private Nose because she had the Sherlock Holmes nose for detection, asked what was wrong.

"It's the ghost!" Amelia's wailed. "I saw it last night, and tonight it's coming to eat me!"

"I don't believe in ghosts," Saturday said. "You'd better tell me what happened."

Jack edged nearer. He was Saturday's assistant, and this sounded like a case for them.

"Ooh!" said Amelia. She stopped crying and bent over Amanda and Miranda. "Uncle Jack's come to say hello to you."

Jack blushed. "Oh, shut up," he said.

"Tell us about the ghost," Saturday said impatiently.

Amelia sat down on the front doorstep, because the grass might be dirty. She put Amanda and Miranda on her lap.

"Well," she said. "You know my bedroom's downstairs, at the back of the house? I was going to sleep last night when I heard this whooing noise. *Whoo, whoo, whoo* — like that. It went on and on. Then the clanking started, like rattling chains. Ugh! And something scratched against the window, like a wild animal trying to get in."

Amelia started to cry again.

Saturday leaned forward. "It couldn't have been a ghost," she said firmly, "because ghosts aren't real. What happened next?"

"My . . . my curtains weren't closed all the

way," cried Amelia. "Suddenly I could see this white shape, and it had two fiery eyes, and it was looking at me."

Jack glanced up at his own house, next door. Suppose the ghost should come and look through *his* bedroom window?

"How tall was it?" Saturday asked.

"I don't know," Amelia said. "Taller than a grown-up, probably. I was so scared I couldn't tell. Anyway, I was trying not to look at it. Then it spoke!"

Jack shivered.

Saturday looked interested. "Well? What did it say?"

Amelia's eyes grew big and round. "It said, 'Tomorrow I'm coming to eat you up, chomp, chomp, chomp. Tomorrow I'm coming to eat you up, chomp, chomp, chomp. Tomorrow — '"

"All right," Saturday said. "I heard you the first time. What was the voice like?"

"Sort of thick and throaty and . . . *hungry!*"

"What did you do?" Jack asked.

"I screamed and ran into the living room," Amelia said. "Daddy looked outside with his flashlight, but he couldn't see anything. He got a little angry because the baby woke up and started crying. Mommy said I must have had a bad dream."

"Maybe you did," Saturday said.

"I didn't!" Amelia shouted. "It was a *real* ghost!"

Saturday sighed. "What do you want me to do?" she asked.

"Catch it! You can catch crooks, so can't you catch a ghost? Go on," Amelia pleaded. "Please. I'll let you play with Amanda and Miranda."

"We'll investigate." Saturday winked at Jack, who immediately felt better. "But I don't want to play with Amanda or Miranda."

The Littlejohns lived nearby, on the road by

*"Daddy looked outside with his flashlight,
but he couldn't see anything."*

the playground. Saturday, Amelia, and Jack went over there right away. Saturday took her brother's magnifying glass. Jack tried to pretend that he wasn't with Amelia, Amanda, and Miranda.

At the Littlejohns' house, Amelia was too scared to go around to the back yard, because that was where the ghost had been.

"You're a sissy," Jack said. "Everyone knows that ghosts don't come out in the daytime."

"They don't come out at all," Saturday said. "Because they're not real."

Amelia decided she would give Miranda and Amanda a tea party in the front yard while Saturday and Jack went around to the back. The back yard was very neat — there were three flowerbeds, a square lawn, a vegetable patch, and a tool shed. Near the shed was a rusty trash can full of dead leaves.

Saturday took out her magnifying glass and

began to crawl over the lawn. It seemed to Jack as though she were looking at every blade of grass.

Jack looked around as well — he didn't see why he couldn't detect something too. But he couldn't find anything except grass and flowers and, after a while, he got bored. Saturday was still on her hands and knees.

"What are you looking for?" Jack asked.

"How can I know," Saturday said, "until I've found it?"

Jack chewed a piece of grass and stared around. On his right was a high brick wall; there was another road on the other side of it. On the left was a tall fence — horrible Ned Knight and his horrible dog Stinker lived in the house beyond.

Next door to the Knights' was the Reillys' house, where Ryan lived. Ryan was a friend of Jack and Saturday's.

He wondered who lived beyond the hedge at the bottom of the Littlejohns' yard. He didn't recognize the house.

"Aha!" said Saturday. She had reached the part of the lawn that was closest to Amelia's bedroom window. "Come and look at this."

Jack rushed over to her. She pointed at two gray blobs on the grass. Neither was larger than Jack's little fingernail.

"What are they?" Jack asked. The blobs looked very unexciting.

"Clues," Saturday said. "Maybe Amelia didn't dream her ghost after all."

She scraped the blobs off the grass and put them in an envelope, which she took from her pocket.

"Why are you doing that?" Jack said.

"You have to keep clues because they prove things."

Saturday refused to tell him why the blobs

43

were important. She went on looking through her brother's magnifying glass. Now she was looking at the plants in the narrow flowerbed directly under Amelia's window.

"Aha!" she said.

Jack looked up. This time he didn't rush over. It wasn't worth rushing for little gray blobs.

Saturday pointed at the rosebush. "Can you see what's here? Hanging on that big thorn?"

Jack came over and had a look. "It's only a piece of white thread," he said. Thread was just as boring as little gray blobs.

Saturday shook her head. "It could be another important clue." She lifted the piece of thread from the thorn and put it in her envelope. "Come on, Jack. Let's look at the rest of the yard."

He trailed after her. She looked very carefully at the wall on the right and at the fence on the left. She looked even more carefully at the hedge at the end of the yard, especially at the part of the hedge that was half hidden by the tool shed.

"*Aha!*" she said, much more loudly than before.

Jack jumped with surprise.

"Come here," she said. "I've found *lots* of clues."

They had to wriggle between the hedge and the shed. Saturday pointed at another piece of white thread that dangled from one of the twigs in the hedge. More excitingly, there was a hole in the hedge. Jack looked through the hole and found that he could see the wooden side of another tool shed. On the ground on the other side of the hole were two more gray blobs.

"Who lives there?" Saturday asked.

Jack shook his head. "I don't know."

"I'm going to investigate," Saturday said.

45

"I'm going to investigate," Saturday said.
She crawled through the hedge and disappeared.

"W-what?" Jack said. "You're going through there?"

Saturday nodded. "Of course."

Jack hoped he didn't look as scared as he was feeling. After all, "through there" was probably where the ghost lived.

"I'll come with you," he said.

To his great relief, Saturday shook her head.

"No," she said. "I'd better go by myself, in case I don't come back. Then you can sound the alarm. Just wait here."

She crawled through the hedge and disappeared. Jack sat on the grass by the tool shed door and closed his eyes tightly. Suppose Saturday didn't come back? Would anyone believe him when he tried to raise the alarm? Suppose the ghost *ate* Saturday? Perhaps the ghost would even eat bones. He reminded himself that ghosts only came out at night, but it no longer sounded as convincing as it had when he said it to Amelia. Suppose —

There was a tap on his shoulder.

Jack gasped and opened his eyes.

Saturday grinned down at him. "You look as if you've seen a ghost!" she said. "Come on, I want to find Amelia."

Jack asked her what she had found out, but she wouldn't say.

Amelia was still giving her dolls their tea in the front yard.

"Have you caught the ghost, Saturday?" she asked. "Have some tea."

Amelia pretended to pour out two cups of tea. She put in pretend milk and sugar and held out the cups to Jack and Saturday. Jack put his down on the grass.

Saturday waved aside the other teacup. "I want some glue," she said. "Then I can deal with your ghost."

"Some *glue?*" Amelia said. "What for?"

"Never you mind," Saturday said.

Amelia went into the house to ask her mother for some glue. In a few minutes she came back with a glue bottle in her hand. Just as she came out, a very fat boy with longish red hair came walking down the road toward the playground. He said nothing, but he stuck out his tongue at Amelia.

"Ugh!" Amelia said as she gave the glue to Saturday. "That mean boy's come back from his uncle's. I wish he'd stayed there forever."

"What's his name?" Saturday said.

"That's Justin Badweather," Jack said.

"He lives in the house behind ours," Amelia said. "Anyway, here's the glue. Mommy said that it takes a long time to dry."

"Good," Saturday said, "that's just what I wanted."

Saturday and Jack went back to the hole in the hedge by the tool shed. Amelia was still too scared to come into the back yard. Once again, Jack stayed on guard while Saturday wriggled through the hedge with the glue bottle in her hand. A few minutes later she returned. She and Jack blocked the hole in the hedge with the old trash can.

"That won't keep out a ghost," Jack said.

Saturday smiled. "It'll keep out this ghost," she said.

They gave back the glue to Mrs. Littlejohn. Amelia wanted to know if they'd caught the ghost.

"Not exactly," Saturday said mysteriously. "But I don't think it'll be causing any more trouble. I'm going down to the playground now. Are you two coming?"

Jack said yes, even though he didn't really want to because Justin Badweather would be there. Amelia said yes because she thought that Amanda and Miranda needed another outing in

*Saturday and Jack blocked the hole in
the hedge with the old trash can.*

their carriage.

When they reached the playground, they found that everyone was standing around the oak tree. Justin Badweather was making a speech to them. Justin sent his friend Ned Knight across to Saturday, Jack, and Amelia, to tell them to come to listen to him.

"Well, I suppose we might as well go and listen," Saturday said. "We've got nothing better to do."

Justin looked at them as they came over. He sneered at Saturday. It was well known that Justin thought all girls were soppy.

"I'm talking about our family ghost," he said importantly. His voice always sounded as if his nose were blocked. "It's my granpa. He died years ago, but people say his ghost still walks around here at night — looking for *food!*"

"*Food?*" said Amelia Littlejohn in a very shaky voice.

Justin nodded. "That's right. His favorite kind of food."

"And what's that?" Ned asked.

"Children!" Justin sniggered. "Tasty little children. My granpa was a sailor, you see. One day he was shipwrecked. My granpa was alone on a raft with two young cabin boys. They had no food. They were rescued two weeks later. At least Granpa was. He was alone and thirty pounds heavier, but the cabin boys were gone."

There was a moment of shocked silence. Justin licked his lips.

"After that," he said, "Granpa always ate children when he got the chance. The younger the better." His eyes rested on Amelia. "Especially little girls."

"Nonsense," said Saturday. "I don't see why girls would taste any different from boys. I don't believe in ghosts, either. Only babies believe in ghosts."

"But I saw it last night," Ned said. "It's dressed in white, and it's got eyes of fire, and it clanks as it walks. Justin's granpa has come back to haunt us."

"You're making it up," Saturday said.

Ned looked away. He was scared of Saturday.

"And who are you?" Justin said. "I don't like new kids, and I don't like girls."

"I'm Saturday Holmes. I'll make you a bet: The person who's pretending to be this ghost will have something wrong with their hair tomorrow morning. That's how we'll know who it is."

Justin's mouth fell open.

Ned said to Justin in a loud whisper, "Better be careful. She's a detective."

"She's just a girl," Justin said. "I'm not scared of no girl. And Saturday's a stupid name."

"I dare you to come here tomorrow, all of

Ned said to Justin in a loud whisper,
"Better be careful. She's a detective."

you," Saturday said, "and see if I'm right."

"I was coming here tomorrow anyway," Justin said. "Tomorrow's Saturday, isn't it? Tell you what, I'm going to clean my shoes on Saturday. Ha, ha, *ha!*"

The next day everyone came to the playground soon after breakfast. They had to come because Saturday had dared them. Also, they wanted to find out whether or not the ghost was real.

Jack was very worried. He couldn't see how Saturday could prove that the ghost wasn't real. And if she couldn't, Justin would have his revenge on Saturday — and on Saturday's friends.

But Saturday wasn't worried. On their way to the playground, they stopped at Amelia's house.

Amelia was very cheerful. "The ghost didn't come last night," she said happily.

"I didn't think it would," Saturday said.

As they passed the Reillys' house, Jack stopped in to ask Ryan to come with them. Ryan was the only person he knew who was strong enough to stand a chance of beating Justin Badweather in a fight. That was one reason why Justin and Ryan were enemies.

The four of them arrived at the playground. Everyone else was already there, except Justin Badweather.

"Never mind," Saturday said. "I can start without him."

She went around and looked carefully at everyone's hair. Jack couldn't understand why. Everyone's hair was exactly the same as it had been yesterday.

Ned Knight said, "I told you so! The ghost is real!"

Suddenly Justin rode into the playground on his big red bike, ringing the bell on the

Saturday went around and looked
carefully at everyone's hair.

handlebars. He stopped just inside the entrance, near where Ryan was standing. He had a very large checked cap on his head.

"Can't stop," he said importantly, "I'm going out with my dad. Haven't got time for your silly games today. I hope the ghost doesn't eat you!"

"Ryan!" Saturday shouted. "Knock his cap off!"

Ryan knocked off Justin's cap. Everyone except Justin started to laugh. Yesterday, Justin's red hair had been long and neatly cut. Now it was short and ragged.

Justin howled with rage, turned his bike, and rode away as fast as he could.

Justin's friends edged away from Saturday and left the playground. Everyone else came closer to her. She was standing by the oak tree, where Justin usually stood.

"I don't understand," Jack said. "How did you do it?"

Saturday shrugged. "It was simple — Justin left so many clues that showed me he was the ghost. The pieces of white thread in Amelia's yard came from the sheet he wore. Those gray blobs were candle wax. When I went through the hedge, I found Justin's ghost disguise in the Badweathers' tool shed. There was an old sheet, a chain to make the clanking noises, and a candle in an empty paint can. He'd cut two holes in the side of the can, which looked like two eyes in the darkness when the candle was lit. Ned Knight must have been in the plot as well."

Ryan frowned. "But what happened to Justin's hair?"

"The sheet was pinned onto an old hat, so it wouldn't fall off." Saturday laughed. "I put the glue inside the hat. Anyone who tried to be a ghost would get glue all over his hair. I bet

Justin's parents had to cut him out with scissors!"

Jack leaned out of bed and
knocked twice on the wall.

THE CASE
OF THE
CAPTURED SHADOWS

Knock. Knock. KNOCK!

Jack Watson sat up in bed and yawned.

Knock. Knock. KNOCK!

Now which signal was that? Luckily the code was on the bedside table. "KNOCK! Knock. Knock": That meant, "The enemy has captured me." Jack rubbed his eyes. Which enemy? That couldn't be right.

Knock. Knock. KNOCK!

He had gotten the wrong signal. "Knock. Knock. KNOCK!" meant, "Meet me outside after breakfast." Perhaps Saturday had another case for them to solve.

Jack leaned out of bed and knocked twice on the wall. That meant, "Message received and understood." Saturday Holmes, the great detective, had the bedroom on the other side of the wall, in the house next door. It was her idea that they should use secret signals to keep in touch.

"Stop that banging!" Jack's father yelled from the next bedroom. "I'm asleep!"

After breakfast Jack went down to the yard. Saturday was already sitting on the wall by the apple tree. Jack climbed up beside her.

"Is it a case?" he asked excitedly.

Saturday shook her head.

Jack felt a little annoyed. If it wasn't a case, why had she signaled for him? Saturday was always being mysterious, even when she had nothing to be mysterious about.

"My brother was telling me about our ancestor Sherlock Holmes last night," she said. "When he'd solved a case, Watson used to say, 'Marvelous, Holmes! How on earth did you do it?' And then Holmes says, 'Elementary, my dear Watson.' I think we should do that."

Jack frowned. "What does elly-whatever-it-was mean?"

"Elementary." Saturday looked down her nose at Jack, as if to say that he should have known what the word meant. "It means you don't understand it but I do. Or something like that."

"But what do you say if *I* solve a case?"

"But you won't, will you?" Saturday jumped down from the wall. "Come on, we've got to practice our detective skills. Let's shadow someone."

Jack nearly said that he wasn't going to come. How could Saturday be so sure he wouldn't solve a case? She was getting bigheaded. On the other hand, he had never shadowed anyone before, and it sounded interesting.

It was. First of all, they had to choose their

disguises. Saturday borrowed her brother's blue jacket. It came down to her knees and it was far too warm for her, but it made her look different. She also wore a pair of sunglasses. Jack found an old straw hat that his mother used in the garden. It flopped over his ears. He carried a comic book that he could pretend to be reading if he needed to hide the rest of his face.

Saturday made sure that they each had a piece of chalk. They might have to split up, and the one in front could draw arrows on the sidewalk to show the way. All they had to do now was choose someone to follow.

"It's better to follow someone who knows us," Saturday said. "It's harder, you see, and we can test our disguises. If we choose someone suspicious, it might even turn into a case for us."

They hid in Saturday's front yard, waiting for someone suspicious to go by. After a few

Mrs. Grump snorted angrily at
the weeds in Mr. Patel's garden.

minutes Mrs. Grump came out of her house on the other side of the road. She snorted angrily at the weeds in Mr. Patel's garden and waddled down the road.

"How about her?" Jack whispered. "She's suspicious all right."

Saturday nodded. "Everyone's scared of her, except me. And I bet she's not really that fat. I bet she's hiding stolen goods under her dress."

Saturday went first. Jack counted up to a hundred before he followed her. At the main road he found a chalked arrow that bent to the right. Mrs. Grump must be going shopping.

When Jack reached the stores he could see no sign of Mrs. Grump. Saturday was standing outside a shoe store. She seemed to be looking at some men's shoes.

Jack tapped her on the shoulder. Saturday jumped.

"Have you lost her?" he asked.

"Of course not! She's in the supermarket. I'm using the shoe store window as a mirror, so I can watch the main entrance. If you go around the corner, you can watch the side door. Find a store window so she won't see that it's you."

Jack went into the side street. There was a toy store opposite the supermarket door. When he stared into its window, he could see the door very clearly. He could also see himself; perhaps his mother's hat was a little large for him.

He waited for what seemed like hours. At least he was outside an interesting store. There was a big red dump truck with a battery-powered electric motor and an orange light that flashed on and off. It looked expensive, but maybe his parents would buy it for his birthday if he went without his allowance for a month.

Just as he was trying to read the price tag, he heard someone grunting behind him. He had been so interested in the toys that he had forgotten to look at the reflection. He glanced around. Mrs. Grump was only a few feet away from him. Jack quickly put up his comic book so she wouldn't recognize him.

Mrs. Grump had a carrier bag in one hand and an airmail envelope in the other. She walked past Jack and into the post office beside the toy store. Jack realized that he was holding the comic book upside down. He was glad that Saturday wasn't there.

He peeped into the post office. Mrs. Grump was waiting in one of the lines. He thought he could guess what she wanted. It was a long line, so he had plenty of time to find Saturday.

She wasn't pleased, and said, "You should never leave a suspect." She rubbed her nose. "An airmail letter! A lot of crooks are international these days."

Jack said, "I bet she was sending it to — "

But Saturday wasn't listening. She was

already running toward the post office. "I'll tail her now," she called over her shoulder. "You wait at the main road and follow me."

Jack shrugged. Saturday was too busy to listen to him. But she wasn't the only one who could have ideas. He stood on the corner and thought how wonderful it would be if he solved a case that had baffled Saturday.

Mrs. Grump came out of the post office. She mailed her letter and shuffled off in the opposite direction, away from where Jack was standing on the main road. Saturday came out of the post office and followed Mrs. Grump. Jack followed Saturday.

The road twisted and turned. Jack lost sight of Saturday. When the road straightened out again, she was nowhere to be seen. But there was a chalk mark on the sidewalk by the gates of the General Warlock Memorial Park.

Jack knew the park, though he didn't go there

very often because it was so boring. It was full of flowerbeds and paths and benches. The trees were too small to climb and you weren't supposed to walk on the grass. The gardener hated dogs and children.

Saturday was crouching beside a trash can. Between the gates and Saturday was a puddle. Jack walked through the water so he could see his footprints on the dry path.

"Don't do that!" Saturday said. "A good shadow never leaves tracks, in case he's being shadowed."

"How was I supposed to know?" Jack demanded. "You never told me that."

"Shhh! Look, the suspect's over there."

Mrs. Grump was talking to the gardener. They were too far away for the detectives to be able to hear what they were saying.

"She's probably telling him where she's going to leave the stolen goods. You know, the ones under her dress. I bet he passes them on to someone else. He looks like a crook."

When Mrs. Grump moved away, Saturday allowed Jack to be the first to follow her. The gardener looked at him very suspiciously as he passed. He said something that sounded like *Grrr!*

Mrs. Grump left the park by the little gate behind the war memorial. Jack followed her into a street of gloomy red brick houses. There were cars parked along the road, so Jack had plenty of cover. Jack didn't recognize the street at first. But one of the houses had a little tower, with stained-glass windows. It looked like a castle. He was almost sure he had seen it before.

Mrs. Grump turned into another street. Jack made a chalk mark on the sidewalk for Saturday. He peered around the corner. The houses here were smaller and even gloomier. Mrs. Grump stopped, looked around, and went

The gardener looked at Jack
very suspiciously as he passed.

into one of the gates near the end of the road.

Jack ran after her. You could hardly see the house (which was number thirteen) because the hedge was so big and untrimmed. There was a FOR SALE notice in the yard. Mrs. Grump had just put a key in the front door. Jack suddenly remembered the one time he had been here before, to this very house.

"Aha!" Saturday whispered. She had come up very quietly behind him. "I thought so. An empty house — it's either the gang's headquarters or where they leave secret messages for one another."

"But — " Jack began.

The front door closed.

"Quick, there's no time to lose," Saturday interrupted. "I'll stay here and watch the front. You scout around to the back of the house. They may try and escape that way."

"They?" Jack said.

*Jack gulped, climbed onto the low
wall, and jumped into the hedge.*

"There may be more than one of them. Go on. You're not scared, are you?"

Jack was, but of course he couldn't admit it. Everyone was scared of Mrs. Grump. He gulped, climbed onto the low wall, and jumped into the hedge.

It was fortunate that no one had done any gardening in that yard for months. In places the grass was as high as Jack's waist. The thick hedge ran along the side of the house, as well as the front, so Jack was able to crawl between it and the wall. He cut his knee twice, and once he ran into some stinging nettles. But he reached the back yard without being spotted by Mrs. Grump. He took cover behind an apple tree and watched the back door.

Mrs. Grump loomed up on the other side of the kitchen window and jerked it open. She said, "Pah! The filth!" and disappeared again.

A minute later Jack heard a bang. It sounded

like someone in a temper closing the front door.

Saturday ran up the path by the side of the house. Jack waved his hat to show her where he was. She flopped down beside him.

"Phew!" she said. "That was a narrow escape. She came out so fast that she nearly caught me. I had to dive into the hedge. I've torn my brother's jacket. Still, now's our chance to find out what she's up to."

"But — "

"You're not still scared, are you?" Saturday stood up. "I'm sure there's no one else in the house. I've been watching it like a hawk."

"No," Jack said. "It's not that. It's — "

"Come on. She's opened the little kitchen window. I bet I can stretch a hand in and open the big one beside it."

"But — "

It was too late. Saturday didn't want to listen to him. She was already climbing onto the windowsill. She reached in and tugged open the handle of the big window. Then she swung herself into the kitchen. Jack followed her in.

"We must move fast," Saturday said. "Keep your eyes peeled for clues. What's that on the floor? Look! It's blood!"

"I know," Jack said glumly. "It's mine."

He had cut his knee as he hauled himself over the sill.

"Then wipe it up with your T-shirt," Saturday hissed. "*We* shouldn't leave clues."

The house had been stripped of furniture. In the hall was Mrs. Grump's carrier bag. Saturday looked in it and found some rags, a new dustpan and brush, and a big bottle of disinfectant.

"She's going to clean up the house and get rid of all the fingerprints and things," she said. "We're just in time."

They looked quickly in each room. All they

found were bare boards and peeling wallpaper. Saturday ran up the stairs with Jack close behind her. The front bedroom was empty. But on the floor of one of the back bedrooms was a yellowing newspaper, folded open at the crossword.

"Aha!" Saturday scooped it up. "Look, only two clues have been written in. You'll never guess what they are."

Jack came closer. "What?"

"One word is POLICE and the other is DISAPPEAR. It's a message, Jack. It means 'The POLICE are on to us. We'd better DISAPPEAR.' Clever, isn't it?"

"But perhaps those words are just the answers," Jack said.

Saturday frowned. " 'Course they aren't. Here's the clue for the POLICE one: 'Work about the insects for the law.' If that means POLICE, I'll eat your hat. The other one, for

DISAPPEAR, is 'Vanish in Hades — a quiet fruit.' That doesn't make sense either. So it must be a secret message."

"But — "

Downstairs, something rattled. The front door banged. A bolt shot back. A muffled "Pah!" floated up the stairs.

Saturday and Jack stared at each other with terror in their eyes. Mrs. Grump had trapped them.

"Pah! All this dirt!"

Mrs. Grump, muttering to herself, began to use the dustpan and brush. Every few seconds, her muttering and the scrape of the brush grew a little louder.

Saturday put her mouth to Jack's ear. "She must be coming up the stairs," she whispered. "Tiptoe behind the door."

One of the floorboards creaked as they moved, but Mrs. Grump appeared not to notice. Jack's heart was pounding so loudly in his chest that he was sure it could be heard all over the house. He tried not to think about what would happen when she caught them. It would probably be even worse than the time Justin Badweather beat him up on the playground. And afterward she would tell their parents.

Saturday clutched Jack's arm. Mrs. Grump had reached the landing. Jack could see her through the crack between the door and the wall. She was panting, and wiping her forehead. She turned and went into the bathroom. There was a gush of running water as she filled up a bucket.

"Quick!" Saturday whispered. "Run!"

They no longer bothered to keep quiet. They hurtled down the stairs, taking three at a time. Saturday tugged at the front door, but it was locked. Jack ran for the kitchen with Saturday

They no longer bothered to keep quiet. They hurtled down the stairs, taking three at a time.

at his heels.

"Who's there?" Mrs. Grump was pounding down the stairs, bouncing like a big black ball. "Stop, thief! Police!"

The door into the kitchen had jammed. Saturday couldn't get it open. Mrs. Grump still hadn't seen them, but it could only be a matter of seconds.

Then Jack had a brainstorm. He opened a little door that was half hidden under the stairs. He grabbed Saturday by the wrist and plunged with her into the darkness beyond.

Jack pushed the door shut behind them. With any luck, Mrs. Grump would think it was the sound of the kitchen door being shut.

It was completely dark. Jack bit his lip and waited.

"Pah!" Mrs. Grump shouted in triumph on the other side of the door. There was a *click!* as she locked them in. "Got you! You won't get out

Jack grabbed Saturday by the wrist and plunged with her into the darkness beyond.

of there in a hurry! We'll see what you have to say to the police! I hope you go to jail!"

The front door banged. The darkness settled around them like a blanket. Saturday tried the door. It was well and truly locked.

She sniffed. "But we're detectives," she said. "We're on the same side as the police. And if she's a crook, why's she going to the police?"

Saturday sniffed again.

Jack coughed. For once he felt as if he were older than Saturday instead of the other way around.

"Put your hand on my shoulder," he said. "We're going down some steps."

Saturday followed him meekly. It was cool in the cellar. At the bottom of the stairs, Jack felt for the wall. Using that as a guide, he worked his way around the cellar, with Saturday close behind him. As he walked, he knocked on the wall. The brick made very little sound.

But suddenly there was the dull boom of wood. Jack reached up and found the bolts. They were stiff and rusty, but he managed to draw them back. Then he pushed. The square of wood fell back and light flooded into the cellar.

Jack pulled himself up into one of the bushes at the side of the house.

"Come on," he said to Saturday. "There's no time to waste. Ow! Watch the nettles!"

Mrs. Grump was talking to Jack's mother over the Watsons' gate.

"You could have knocked me down with a feather," Mrs. Grump screeched. "There were two burglars. I only caught a glimpse of them, out of the corner of my eye. Huge, evil-looking men. I think they wore masks. But they didn't get much change out of me. Pah! I locked them in the cellar and called the police from next door."

"So they've been arrested?" Mrs. Watson asked.

Mrs. Grump wobbled with indignation. "The police took hours! I could have been murdered! By the time they arrived, the crooks had escaped. Pah!"

"Did they find any clues?" Mrs. Watson asked.

"I found the clues," Mrs. Grump said firmly. "Two of them. A pair of sunglasses and a great big straw hat. 'You mark my words,' I told the police, 'those burglars are foreigners.' "

Jack, who had been standing on his head behind his mother's back and pretending not to listen, turned himself the right way up and walked quietly down the path to the back yard.

Saturday was already waiting on the wall. They hadn't had time to talk since their escape. They had split up and gone home as quickly as possible, by different ways.

"You were wonderful, Jack," she said. "I mean, it was dark in that cellar. You must have x-ray eyes."

Jack climbed up the apple tree and sat beside her on the wall. For a moment he wondered if he should tell her everything. He had tried to tell her several times, but Saturday just wouldn't listen. He could have told her that Mrs. Grump's married sister had gone to Australia last winter, and that Mrs. Grump was always sending her airmail letters; that they used to live in that empty house near the park; that Jack had gone there once, for the birthday party of Mrs. Grump's nephew; that they'd played hide-and-seek all over the house; and that he knew all about the empty cellar, because Justin Badweather had left the party early through the old coal hatch, taking the birthday cake with him.

"How on earth did you do it?" Saturday asked.

Jack smiled mysteriously. "Elly . . . er, elementary," he said. "Elementary, my dear Holmes."